Published by PI Kids, an imprint of Phoenix International Publications, Inc.

8501 West Higgins Road	34 Seymour Street	Heimhuder Straße 81
Chicago, Illinois 60631	London W1H 7JE	20148 Hamburg

PI Kids is a trademark of Phoenix International Publications, Inc., and is registered in the United States.

www.pikidsmedia.com

ISBN: 978-1-5037-6163-6

QUINN B. QUOKKA
RIDES THE WAVES

WRITTEN BY RACHEL HALPERN
ILLUSTRATED BY ERIC SCALES

pi kids®

An imprint of Phoenix International Publications, Inc.

Chicago • London • New York • Hamburg • Mexico City • Sydney

Quinn B. Quokka hopped across the dunes with his best friends, Billie and Hugo, while he explained his latest plan.

"...and once I get the Prime Minister to announce National Quokka Day," Quinn said, "I'll—whoa, what's going on?"

The familiar beach was full of unfamiliar faces.

Quinn saw athletes from all across Australia. Big kangaroos were lifting weights. Speedy wallabies were having hopping races. And a dingo in fancy sunglasses was showing off in front of the judge's table.

Billie spotted a poster. "Rottnest Island Surfing Contest," she read. "Winner gets a whale-watching tour!"

Quinn could picture it: Surfing to victory. Making friends with whales around the globe. Becoming a world-famous whale expert! "I'm going to win that contest," Quinn said.

"But Quinn," Hugo asked anxiously. "Do you know how to surf?"

"Well, no. But don't worry!" said Quinn with a grin. "I have a plan."

Billie sighed. "Here we go again..."

As Quinn described his victory plan, he slipped on a bottle of sunscreen. "Whoops!" He toppled over and hit a surfboard... which hit another board...which hit the lifeguard tower...which hit the judge's table. Soon, nothing on the beach was left standing!

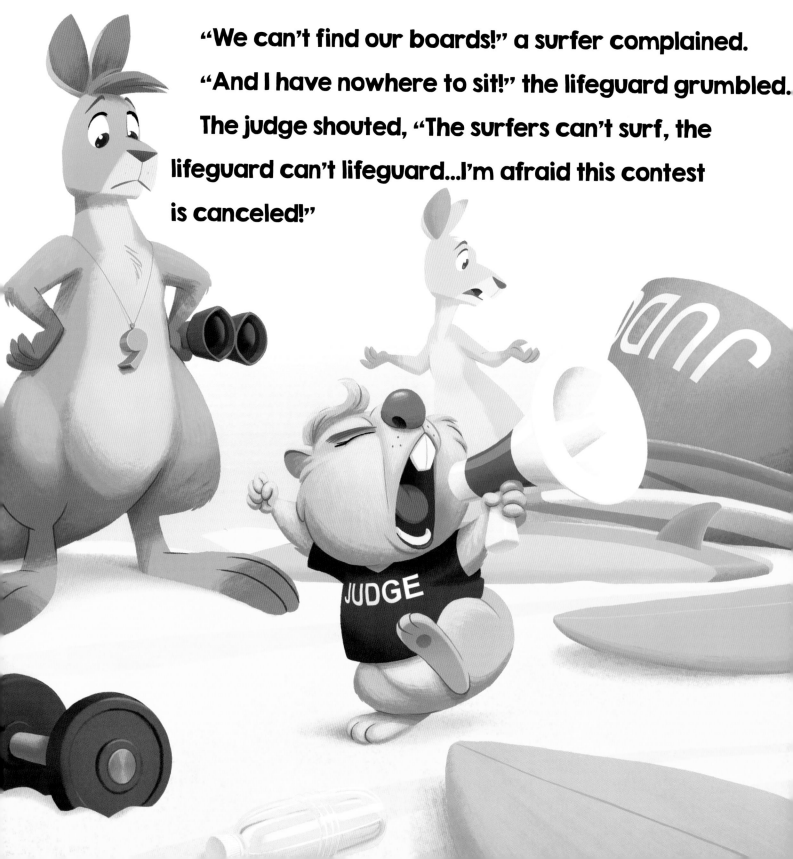

"We can't find our boards!" a surfer complained. "And I have nowhere to sit!" the lifeguard grumbled. The judge shouted, "The surfers can't surf, the lifeguard can't lifeguard...I'm afraid this contest is canceled!"

"So," Quinn told his friends, "this might, possibly, be partly my fault. But I will fix it! Because—"

"Don't say it," Billie said.

"—I have a plan!" said Quinn with a grin.

"I hate it when he says that," Hugo whispered.

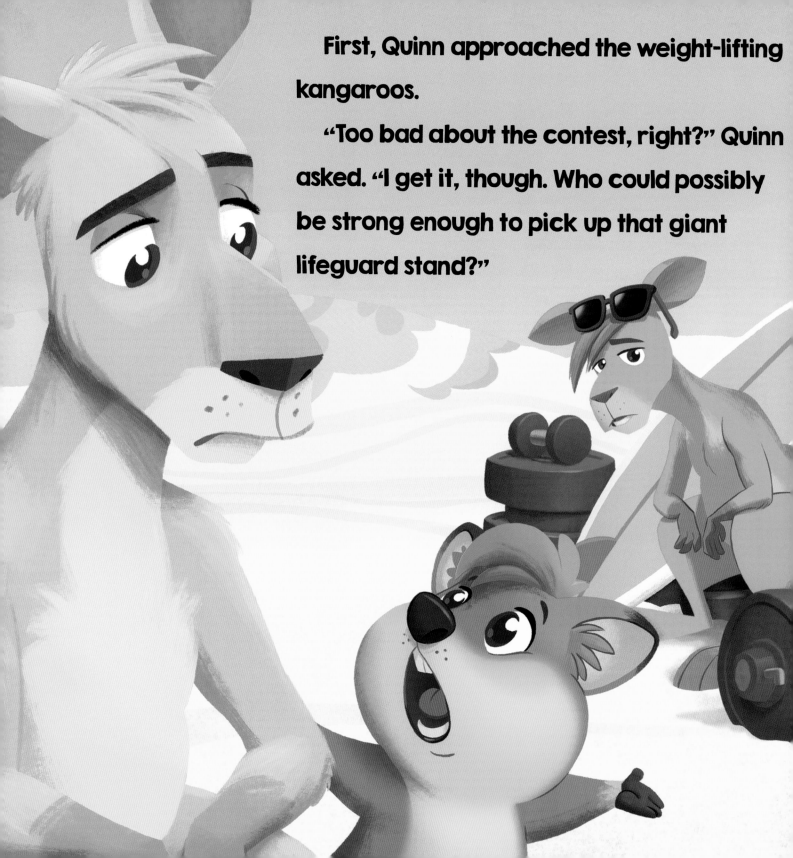

First, Quinn approached the weight-lifting kangaroos.

"Too bad about the contest, right?" Quinn asked. "I get it, though. Who could possibly be strong enough to pick up that giant lifeguard stand?"

Next, Quinn found the wallabies he'd seen racing.

"There are so many surfboards," Quinn said. "It would take someone really, really fast to sort them all out before the contest is supposed to start."

With no audience to admire him, the stylish dingo sat sadly on a fallen board.

Quinn strolled past, saying loudly, "If only someone could put the judge's table back, I bet she'd be super impressed!"

Soon, the contest was back on!

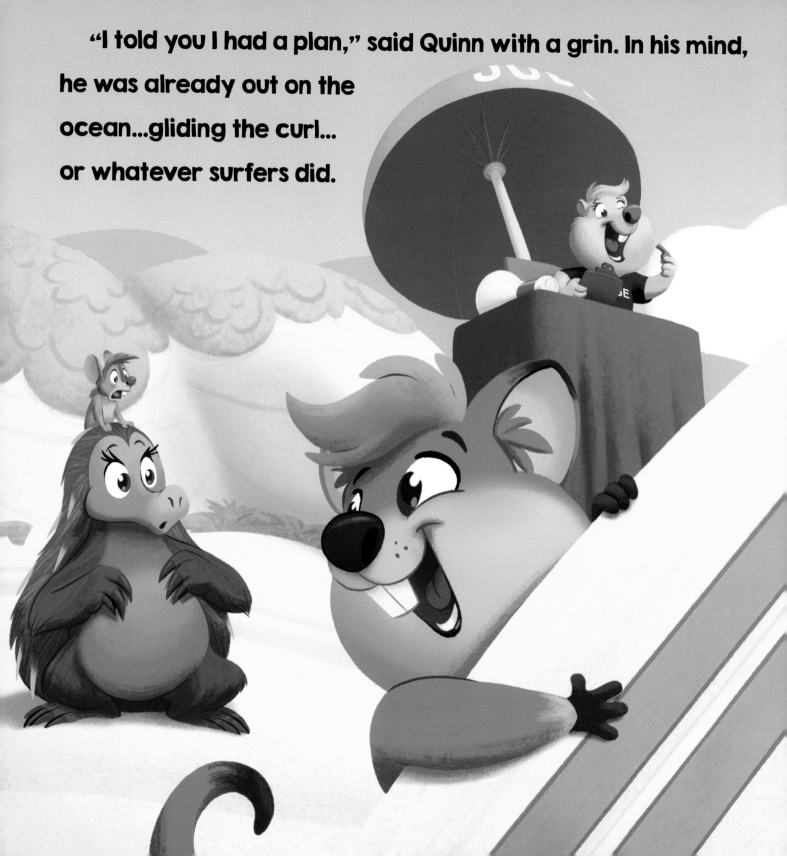

"I told you I had a plan," said Quinn with a grin. In his mind, he was already out on the ocean...gliding the curl... or whatever surfers did.

As Quinn grabbed a board and headed for the starting line, Billie called after him, "But you still don't know how to surf!"

The whistle blew.

Quinn jumped up onto his surfboard—and immediately tumbled off.

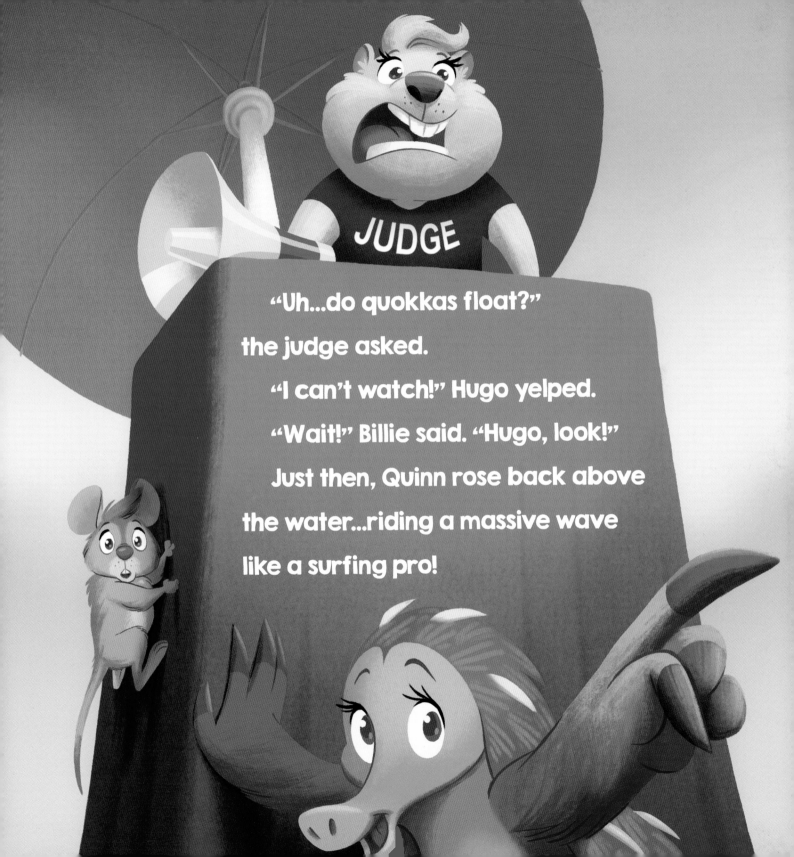

"Uh...do quokkas float?" the judge asked.

"I can't watch!" Hugo yelped.

"Wait!" Billie said. "Hugo, look!"

Just then, Quinn rose back above the water...riding a massive wave like a surfing pro!

As Quinn got closer, everyone could see that he wasn't standing on a surfboard. He was riding on the back of a humpback whale!

Quinn hopped off, beaming. "Thanks for the lift!" he called.

A deep voice answered, "No worries, little quokka. Anytime."

"So, did I win?" Quinn asked.

"No, you were disqualified," Billie said. "I guess a whale doesn't count as a surfboard."

"Oh, well," Quinn said. "I don't need the tour, now that I have a whale for a best mate!" He could picture it: Riding the waves on his new bestie's back...

"Hmmmph," said Billie.

"Second-best mate!" Quinn said. "Third-best. Just a pen pal!"

As he hopped home, Quinn drafted the letter in his head:

Dear Whale Pal, I just came up with the most amazing plan...

Meet the Quokka!

Quokkas can only be found in one small area of the world, so it's important to care for them and their habitat! These charming, tree-climbing animals live mainly on Rottnest Island off the western coast of Australia.

These selfie stars are beloved for their curious, friendly nature and their "smile," which has earned them the nickname "happiest animal on earth"!